MIRACULOUS

DIVISHA SHARMA

Copyright © Divisha Sharma
All Rights Reserved.

This book has been self-published with all reasonable efforts taken to make the material error-free by the author. No part of this book shall be used, reproduced in any manner whatsoever without written permission from the author, except in the case of brief quotations embodied in critical articles and reviews.

The Author of this book is solely responsible and liable for its content including but not limited to the views, representations, descriptions, statements, information, opinions and references ["Content"]. The Content of this book shall not constitute or be construed or deemed to reflect the opinion or expression of the Publisher or Editor. Neither the Publisher nor Editor endorse or approve the Content of this book or guarantee the reliability, accuracy or completeness of the Content published herein and do not make any representations or warranties of any kind, express or implied, including but not limited to the implied warranties of merchantability, fitness for a particular purpose. The Publisher and Editor shall not be liable whatsoever for any errors, omissions, whether such errors or omissions result from negligence, accident, or any other cause or claims for loss or damages of any kind, including without limitation, indirect or consequential loss or damage arising out of use, inability to use, or about the reliability, accuracy or sufficiency of the information contained in this book.

Made with ♥ on the Notion Press Platform
www.notionpress.com

Dedicated to my guiding stars, Mom and Dad, whose unwavering love and support have illuminated every step of my journey. To my beloved little brother Saatvik, whose laughter brings joy to our lives and whose presence fills our hearts with warmth. Your love and encouragement inspire me to believe in the miraculous. With deepest gratitude and endless love, this book is dedicated to you.

Contents

Foreword

Welcome to the exhilarating world of "Miraculous." Within the pages of this captivating book, you'll embark on an extraordinary journey to the vibrant streets of Paris, France, where two remarkable superheroes tirelessly fight to protect their beloved city from the clutches of evil.

At the heart of this tale lies the enigmatic figure of Hawkmoth, a formidable adversary whose thirst for power knows no bounds. With cunning and malevolence, Hawkmoth orchestrates a series of nefarious schemes, crafting and summoning villains of unparalleled menace, all in a relentless pursuit to seize the miraculous abilities of our valiant heroes.

As you delve into the pages of "Miraculous," prepare to be swept away by a whirlwind of adventure, courage, and friendship. Join our heroes as they navigate the perilous challenges of heroism, confronting not only the external threats that loom large over Paris but also the internal struggles that test the very essence of their identities.

So, dear reader, fasten your seatbelt and brace yourself for an unforgettable odyssey into the heart of heroism. For in the world of "Miraculous," miracles are the product of unwavering determination, unyielding courage, and the indomitable spirit of those who dare to believe in the extraordinary.

With warmest regards,
Divisha Sharma

Preface

Within the expansive universe of "Miraculous Ladybug," where ordinary lives intertwine with extraordinary destinies, this book serves as a beacon of illumination, shedding light on the valiant exploits of two superheroes who stand as guardians of their beloved city.

As enthusiasts of the "Miraculous Ladybug" series will attest, the bond between our intrepid heroes transcends mere camaraderie—it is forged in the crucible of shared purpose, unwavering resolve, and a steadfast commitment to protect the innocent from the machinations of evil.

In the hallowed streets of their urban playground, our heroes confront the looming specter of their arch-nemesis, the nefarious Hawkmoth. With his sinister designs and insidious powers, Hawkmoth emerges as a formidable adversary, whose malevolent schemes threaten to plunge the city into darkness.

Yet, amidst the chaos and uncertainty, hope flickers like a beacon in the night. Through the indomitable courage and selfless sacrifice of our heroes, the light of justice shines ever brighter, illuminating the path to redemption and triumph.

So, dear reader, prepare to embark on an exhilarating journey into a world where the extraordinary becomes the norm and where the indomitable spirit of heroism reigns supreme.

With gratitude and hope,
Divisha

Acknowledgements

Writing "Miraculous" has been a journey filled with countless moments of inspiration, support, and encouragement. I am deeply grateful to all those who have contributed to the creation of this book and have helped bring its vision to life.

First and foremost, I would like to express my heartfelt gratitude to my family – Mom, Dad, and Saatvik – for their unwavering love, encouragement, and understanding throughout this journey. Your belief in me has been my greatest source of strength and inspiration.

I am indebted to my friends and colleagues who have offered their support and encouragement, providing valuable feedback and insights that have enriched the pages of this book. Your friendship and camaraderie have made this journey all the more rewarding.

To my editor and publishing team, thank you for your guidance, expertise, and dedication to this project. Your passion for storytelling and commitment to excellence have helped shape "Miraculous" into the book it is today.

Finally, to the readers – thank you for embarking on this journey with me. It is my sincere hope that the book will touch your hearts, spark your imagination, and remind you of the miracles that surround us every day.

With deepest gratitude,
Divisha Sharma

Prologue

Characters

ᐳᐳᐳ

Marinette Dupain-Cheng

Marinette is a sweet and kind girl who loves to design and expel her ideas of creativity.

Adrien Agreste

Kwami-Plagg

Superhero-CatNoir
Wanting to be - A model (Being forced by his father)
Likes - Hanging out with friends

Gabriel Agreste

Kwami-Nooroo

Supervillain-Hawk Moth
Wanting to be - the most powerful person

Alya Césaire

Kwami-Trixx

Superhero-Rena Rouge
Wanting to be- Vlogger
Likes-Making videos about Ladybug

Nathalie Sancoeur

Gabriel's Assistant
(Might have a miraculous in the future)

ONE

A SCHOOL HOLIDAY!

"**H**-hi Adrian!" Marinette struggled. "Hey, how are you? I haven't seen you in days!" Exclaimed Nino.

"Hey, everyone. I'm fine, though" Adrian replied. "Where were you, all these days Adrian?" Asked Alya. "Umm..Well... I had to go to my aunt's house as my father had some work there".

Said Adrian. "Wow, it looks like you have a busy dad!" Yelled Nino.

"Yeah.." Adrian replied. "Wait!" Said Alya. "What happened?" said Nino. "Where's Marinette?" Alya panicked. Nino shrugged in reply. "Um... Marinette was right here." Adrian processed.

"We should find her!" Alya yelled as if her feet were off the ground. Nino then pointed out on a small wooden cruise. "How about we go on that cruise? Not for fun! Only to find Marinette," Nino suggested. "Hmmm... ok." Alya and Adrian thought and looked at each other.

"Yes, I remember! That is the place where Luka plays his guitar the whole day!" Alya processed. "Let's go now," Adrian had no other option but to advise. Then, all of them went on that small wooden cruise. "Oh hey, Luka!" Said Alya.

"Hey, Alya," Luka said in a gentle tone. "Marinette, where were you? Why are you here?" Alya asked a lot of questions which left Marinette with an annoyed frown. "I know," She replied.

"A bee stung me, and I was so irritated!-" Marinette struggled but she was then interrupted by Alya, trying to calm her down.

She sat beside Marinette, "Now tell me what happened," Said Alya as she saw the bee sting that was swollen on her hand. "Aww ... that bee-stung might hurt you a lot, right?" Alya pouted.

Marinette nodded and said, "I came to Luka, and he played a beautiful song for me on the guitar and tried to forget that bee sting". "Well, that's nice of you, Luka," Said Nino. "Yeah, thanks, I guess.." Said Adrian. "Thanks, guys, I really appreciate your compliments," Said Luka.

"Wait!" Said Nino. "What's wrong with you now, Nino?" Alya said as she was really furious with him. "Don't we have school today?" Nino panicked. "You just realised it now? Today is a holiday." Said Alya.

"Yay!" Yelled Nino, "A school holiday!" Adrian and Nino both started dancing and shouted a really weird song.

"A school holiday, a school holiday..." Nino shouted and didn't even realise that he accidentally pushed Adrian off the bridge, into the lake.

Both Ayla and Marinette started laughing at Adrian, and when he started to get out of the water, he was covered in seaweed and was really cold.

Marinette started to worry and had a lot of thoughts in her mind like- "What will happen to him? Will he get a cold? Should I help him? Or no?" Marinette was really confused. "Hey guys," Said Marinette. "What's wrong, girl?" Asked Alya.

"Ummm... It's getting dark, right?" Asked Marinette. "Yes, why?" Asked Nino. "Guys, it's getting dark, I guess we should go home right?" Said Adrian. All of them agreed and went home..But for Adrian, he sang a song about his mother.

His mother passed away when he was just three years old. His father has taken a really difficult job, which would stress him out. "What if I tried my father's job and see how hard it is?" Adrian ran home with a small torch and snuck into his father's office. He looked along for anything he could find. Suddenly, a weird coloured file dropped on the floor. "SMASH!"

"Opps... great now I'm dead." He muttered. He looked through the same file and at last, he had a photo of someone.

Some with a silver type mask and a purple butterfly in front of his eyes.

"Who is he?"Adrian was trying to get an image of him in his mind but failed.

A few seconds later, he heard some footsteps coming towards him. It's getting louder and louder and louder.. "Oh no, looks like I'm grounded for a month now."

He feared. He stood there in silence and saw a flash of light from the window and thought that he could jump out from the window, he looked out the window and jumped.

His dad came in and saw his file on the floor. He picked it up and started thinking about who could do such a thing, while Adrian was peeking through the window. After a few moments, he saw his father walking out of the office.

Adrien then started climbing up to his room with the help of two ladders one over the other.

As he was climbing those ladders, he noticed that those ladders were shaking and were about to fall. He then got a hold of his window and BAAM, those ladders fell down super loud.

Adrien's father and his caretaker named 'Nathalie', both came running down the stairs and saw those ladders on the ground.

Adrian quickly climbed up and closed the windows of his room and peeked at them and saw them going back inside.

Adrien sighed and went to sleep.

It was around 2 a.m., and he heard a noise from downstairs. It sounded like something heavy had fallen down. It lasted just for a couple of seconds then, it was all still.

Adrien got up from his bed and walked up to his bedroom door.

He leaned on to the door and tried to listen to what was going on. Nathalie opened the door from the outside and Adrien fell down to the ground.

"You should have gone to sleep now Adrien". Said Nathalie.

"What was that sound? And why are you awake, it's 2 a.m?" Adrien asked. Nathalie ignored his question and walked outside of the room. "You must be asleep when I come again".

Nathalie said and walked away. Adrien had a big frown on his face. He crawled up on his bed, still thinking about the noise.

Adrien blinked his eyes a few times and went back to sleep.

TWO

THE FOREIGN FESTIVAL

"Hey, guys!" Yelled Nino and gave a high-five to Alya and Marinette.

"Where's Adrian? Did he forget that today is his favourite festival?!" Said Alya. "No, no, no Alya!" Said Nino as he tried to calm down Alya and did a body-language that Adrian will come later. "Oh, he's dead if he doesn't come!" Yelled Alya. "Yeah, yeah! You can even kill him if he doesn't show up this time!" Said Nino.

"Mari? What's wrong? Why are you so gloomy?" Asked Alya in a gentle voice. "I-is L-Luka coming?" Asked Marinette.

Then comes Luka, he creeps behind Marinette and... "BOO!", "AHH!! A Monster! Alya Help!" Yelled Marinette "Please don't kill me! I'm too young to die!".

Nino and Alya both covered their mouths and tried to control their laughter. "Pttf! Hahaha!" Luka laughed so much that he started to bring tears to his eyes.

"Luka! Oh, you're dead!"

Marinette scolded Luka but Luka didn't care. He was still laughing at Marinette "You should have seen your face! Haha!".

"Oh, there comes Adrian!" Said Nino. "Hey, guys! Sorry, I had to come late, and by the way, did I miss anything?" Asked Adrian as he came running down the street.

"Hey, bro, and no you just came on time! Everyone was waiting for you!" Said Nino. "Ok people! Is anyone else missing around here?" Asked Alya. "No!" Said the crowd and were just about to light up the fireworks.

Soon, all of them were lit and those fireworks were so colorful and beautiful that Marinette couldn't take her eyes off them!

"Those fireworks are so beautiful!" Said Marinette in a very excited tone. "Mhm! They are!" Alya replied as she hugged Marinette tightly. "What's wrong?" Asked Marinette. "Nothing, just... thanks for coming, girl!" Said Alya.

"I couldn't miss this opportunity!" Marinette replied as she watched the fireworks. Soon, all the fireworks were finished.

"Aww... the fireworks are finished! I wanted to see those things more!" Said Nino.

"Shut up, Nino! Do you just want to see those things forever, or do you even want to party?" Said Alya as she dragged Nino to the café. "Hey! Stop dragging me, Alya! You know I can walk!" Said Nino and was trying to get free from Alya's hands. "So... uh, what do you wanna do, Marinette?" Asked Adrian in a gentle voice.

"Maybe u-uh shall we go to the p-park?" Marinette struggled. "Sure!" Said Adrian. Both of them went to the park and sat beside the fountain. "Now what?" Asked Marinette.

"How about we talk for a while about your classes and test results and that kind of stuff," said Adrian. "Ok!" Said Marinette, and they both started talking. They got so deep into their conversation that they didn't even notice that 3 hours had passed!

Then Adrian checked his watch and said, "Oh My God!" Said Adrian in a panic mode. "What?" Said Marinette. "3 hours have passed, and we didn't even notice!" Said Adrian.

"Oh no! I had to bake a cake for this festival! I hope my parents baked it!"

Said Marinette in a panic mode. "You should go home now Mari" Said Adrian as he got up and stretched.

"Ok, bye Adrian! It was nice talking to you!" Said Marinette and she waved goodbye to Adrian. "Bye Mari!" Said Adrian and walked home.

Marinette waved at Alya and Nino but they were so busy in their conversation and didn't even notice that it was night time! "Seriously!?" Said Marinette and thought

"They are way too busy in their conversations! They didn't even see me!? I'll just go home" and Marinette went home.

"Hey Alya, it's getting dark, we should go home," said Nino. Alya nodded and they both went home but... they were still chatting.

"So Marinette, everyone left so I guess we should too". Said Adrian.

"Y-yeah, we should". Marinette stood up and walked home. Adrien as well stood up and rushed home.

THREE
SICKNESS

Marinette had a high fever.

She is so sick that she can't even get out of her bed, "Marinette sweetie, what's wrong?" Marinette's mom, 'Sabine' said as she brought some medicines with her from the kitchen from downstairs.

Marinette didn't have the energy to get up and drink her medicine. "You need to skip school and go to the doctor!" Said Sabine and then her father 'Tom' came to her daughter's room. "What's wrong?" Said Tom as he hugged Marinette, "Mari!

You have a high fever!" Said Tom. Marinette nodded and tried to get up but couldn't because of her weakness. "We need to go to the hospital," said Sabine.

"Let's go! Hurry!" Said Tom in a panic mode. Then, Marinette had to skip school and go to the hospital. She was thinking about going to a beach instead of going to a doctor!

She is always very petrified of some of the doctors. They were about to get into their car, and suddenly their car wasn't opening!

Their car doors were like if someone had stuck some super-duper glue on it!

"Seriously! Why isn't it opening!?" Said Sabine in a panic mode "Tom? Can you please get some warm water?" "Sure!" Said Tom and rushed to the kitchen,

while Marinette was thinking...

"Phew! Good thing the car isn't opening! I'm safe! This should take a while, though".

"Got the warm water!" Said Tom running from the kitchen.

Sabine then pointed out to the car and did a body-language to pour the warm water on the sides and the edges of the car doors.

"It worked! We can go to the hospital now!" Said Tom as he flashed to open the doors. "Tom! Are you forgetting something?"

Said Sabine with a brief smile. Tom's eyebrows shot up and said, "No? Or did I?" Tom was so puzzled that he had never been that puzzled in his life!

"The keys!?" Said Sabine in a grave tone. "How will a car start without the keys!?" "Oh sorry! I'll bring it!" Said Tom and rushed to his bedroom.

"Can we just go already?! Said Sabine. *Cough cough* Marinette coughed badly.

Till then, Tom brought the key and they sat in their car and rode to the hospital.

After 15 minutes, they arrived at their destination and told Marinette to walk inside the hospital and wait for them while Sabine and Tom tried to remove the super-'duper' glue.

"Finally! We removed this stupid glue!" Said Sabine and rushed to Marinette. "Mom? What is the time?" Asked Marinette.

"Let me check," Said Sabine as she grabbed her phone and looked at the time.

She showed it to Marinette that the time was 1:56 p.m. *Ring ring!* Sabine's phone started to ring and told Marinette to stay here till her father came in.

"Marinette sweetie, I got to go outside for a phone call. Stay here till your father comes in. Ok?" Said Sabine and went outside and started talking.

"I'm here!" Said Tom as he came running from the car. "Where is your mom sweetie?" "Mom is talking-on the-phone". Said Marinette. Tom then checked Marinette's fever by keeping his hand on her forehead.

"Your fever is low!

"Said Tom in delight. "Really?" Said Marinette and after saying this, her name was called out to meet the doctor. "Here's your medicine…"

Said the doctor and gave Marinette her pills. "Please take it on time".

"Ok!" Said Marinette as her mother came into the room. "Will she be alright?" Said Sabine and she checked Marinette's fever.

"Yes ma'am," Said the doctor.

"Can we go now??" Said Tom in a worried voice. "Sure sir," Said the doctor and told Marinette to take her pills every day.

Marinette thanked the doctor and went home.

FOUR

A MEETING WITH THE KWAMIES

"Oh no, I'm late!" Said Marinette and rushed to the front door.

"Wait!" Said Sabine and held Marinette's hand. "Yes, mom?" Said Marinette.

"You forgot your macaroons!"

Said Sabine and gave Marinette the macaroons and told her to give it to her classmates.

"Bye, mom!" Said Marinette as she rushed outside and saw an old man crossing the road, but the signal was green and the vehicles were going across him.

Marinette saw a large truck that was coming at an awful high speed and she ran to the old man and pushed him to the other side of the road.

"Oh my god! Thank you, darling! You saved my life!" Said the old man and stood up.

"You're welcome, sir!" Said Marinette as she stood up and helped the old man and offered him the macaroons that she had.

"Would you like to have some of my macarons sir?"

Said Marinette but the old man refused and asked where she was going to take the macaroons.

"I-I am going to take these macaroons to school!" Said Marinette and told him that she was late for school.

The old man said goodbye to her and when Marinette looked back to say one last goodbye, the old man was not there!

"Where did he go?" Marinette said this to herself and ran to school.

The school gates were about to close and Marinette came just on time and she ran to class. "Where is the teacher?" Asked Marinette.

"Sorry, class! I'm a little late!" Said the class teacher 'Ms. Bustier'. "Okay, class!" "Where's Adrian?" Asked Nino.

"He didn't come again, Nino. Please get back to work." Said Ms. Bustier and told everyone to open their books. While with Adrian.....

Why can't I just go to school?" Said Adrian.

"I'm sorry Adrian, but you're not allowed to go to school because your father has gotten a lot busier" Said Adrian's Caretaker 'Nathalie'.

"It's useless then, You can go, Nathalie!" Said Adrian in an angry tone while Nathalie left his room silently.

Adrian started to think like... "Why can't I go anywhere!? I can't go to school! I can't go anywhere! I don't want to be homeschooled again!" "Should I escape and go to school? I can jump out of the window though"

Adrian thought of a plan.

He started to make a recording of himself in his room, reading a book and eating.

Adrian then jumped out of the window and ran to school.

"Adrian... Adrian? Are you in your room?"

Said Nathalie as she rushed to his room and saw the recording on the radio. "Ugh! He escaped!! Bodyguard!

Drive us to Adrian's school!" Said Nathalie and rushed to the car and started it.

After a while, they reached and Adrian was just about to enter the school and then, Nathalie stopped him and told him to stay home but Adrian refused and saw an old man who was walking and tripped on his own feet and his walking stick was far away from him.

Adrian ran to the old man and forgot about Nathalie's words and helped the old man to get up. "Thank You, young man," Said the old man.

"You're welcome, sir!" Said Adrian and went back to Nathalie.

"You did a good thing Adrian," Said Nathalie and told him that he can continue to go to school and Nathalie will have a talk with Adrian's father 'Gabriel'.

"Thanks, Nathalie!" Thought Adrian and rushed to school. "I'm late! I'm so sorry" Adrian said in a panic as he came running down the stairs. "It's alright Adrian! Now, get back to work people!" Said Ms. Bustier

After School....

"Finally! I can go to school!" Adrian said to himself. Just then, a mysterious type of small box appeared in front of him. The same thing happened with Marinette! She was swinging in her study table chair and a box appeared in front of her too! They both opened them and a mouse looking type of 'creatures' appeared.

"Hi!" Said the first creature of Marinette. "I'm Tikki! I'm your kwami!" Said the creature as it rushed hither and thither. "AHHH! WHAT ARE YOU!? A MICE! NO BUG-MICE!!"

Marinette struggled as she threw some boxes, containers, and crumbled papers. "Marinette, you are the chosen one! You are meant to protect the city!" Said Tikki.

While with Adrian...

Yawns "Hi! I'm Plagg!" Said the creature. "Wow! Are you the ones of the creatures that transform us into whatever we wanna become?"Asked Adrian. "No, no, no! Adrian! I'm your kwami! I can transform you into superheroes!" Said Plagg. *Sniffs* "What's that smell?" Asked Plagg. "Oh, this? This is camembert!" Said Adrian and showed it to Plagg. "Wow... this is the most beautiful thing I've ever seen!" Said Plagg and started to eat that thing from Adrian.

"So, what do I say then?" Asked Adrian.

"Oh! You just have to say, Plagg! Claws out! Ok?"

Said Plagg and continued to eat again. "Alright! Plagg! Claws out!" Said Adrian and started to transform. "Wow! Plagg? Where are you? Should I jump outside Plagg? I kinda, um... transformed into a cat type superhero."

Adrian Asked Plagg many times but there was pin-drop silence.

Adrian thought of going outside cause he had a cat costume and a really long stick that had a cat pawed print on it and can also adjust the size too! Adrian went to the window and jumped to another building and the other!

"Wow! I can jump so high!" Then he put his 'cat stick type of rod' between two buildings and started to walk on it even though the stick was thin.

While with Marinette... "What do I say then, Tikki?" Asked Marinette. "You have to say, Tikki! Spots on! Ok?" Said Tikki.

"Spots on?" Said Marinette and she started to transform. "W-what is this!?" Marinette said it in a panic mode.

"Tikki? Tikki? Where are you?" Asked Marinette and just then, Sabine was calling Marinette but she couldn't go 'because she had this 'funny' costume. Marinette ran to the balcony upstairs and she also had a weird thing like a 'yoyo'.

She started to think that she could swing really high. And she did! She attached the 'yoyo' to a dog type statue and pulled.

She didn't know what's gonna happen next! She pulled it and she started to go hither and thither.

"Aaa!!" Marinette yelled so loud that other people saw her! They started to say things like, "Wow! Look! A Superhero!" Said one of the citizens. Then, she met Adrian walking on his thin rod and Marinette fell on him!

But, they can't tell who they are. "Hi!" Said Marinette "Who are you?" asked Adrian. "I'm" Marinette struggled.

"I'm Ladybug!" Said Marinette and Adrian told his name "I'm Cat Noir! Nice to meet you Ladybug!" Said Cat Noir.

"Ok, So... what do we do now?" Asked Ladybug. "I guess we get to know each other more?" Asked Cat Noir "We can't!" Said Ladybug.

"And why's that?" Asked Cat Noir as he went on to the Eiffel tower. "I'm not done yet!" Said Ladybug and rushed behind Cat Noir.

"We can't tell our identities to someone Kitty!" Said Ladybug. "It's a secret and if you told your identities to someone then, I'll get to know who you are!" Said Ladybug and went home.

"Bye Ladybug..." Said Cat Noir and rushed home.

FIVE

WELL HELLO, FIRST SUPER VILLAIN.

"Oh Tikki! I'm late again!" Rushed Marinette in a hurry. "Where's your mom and dad Marinette?"

Asked Tikki. "Ooh, I remember! They went to the grocery store for food." Said Marinette "Wait! Where will you hide Tikki? Someone might see you."

Marinette rushed upstairs and grabbed a small purse without any pockets. Just a golden hock that opens the small purse.

"Let's go Marinette! You're late!" Tikki said it in a panic. Marinette told Tikki to go and hide inside the small purse and Marinette rushed to school.

Marinette was just running and she suddenly stopped. "What's wrong Marinette?" Asked Tikki. "Uh-oh, how could I forget this day?" Marinette started to panic and she was trying to tell Tikki that today was 'the special day'.

Tikki was crossed.

"I can't understand whatever you are saying.." Said Tikki. "Today is Alya's birthday! How could I forget it?" Said Marinette and told Tikki that she will go to school and make something for Alya there.

Tikki agreed and they went to school. When she reached, Marinette saw Alya with a long face and tears running down her face.

Marinette approached her and looked at her with the eyes of some kind of guilt. "What's wrong Alya?" Marinette asked politely.

"Do you know what day it is today?" Asked Alya and she cried and put her head on Marinette's shoulder.

Marinette pretended to forget what day it was.

"You too..?" Said Alya and started weeping silently. "What's wrong Alya?" Asked Nino in a gentle voice. "Did you forget what day it is?"

Said Alya in an angry voice. Nino was crossed. "What are you talking about, today's Wednesday, did you forget or did I forget something?" Said Nino.

Alya rushed towards the school restroom and locked herself in. "Nino, did you forget what day it is?" Marinette whispered. "No, I lied 'cause I wanted to surprise her." Said Nino and left for his class.

"I can feel the pain of that little girl..." Said a man in a deep voice.

That person was named, 'Hawk Moth'.

He was Adrian's father named "Gabrial Agreste". He also had a kwami called "Nooroo". Gabriel went into his office where no one was allowed to enter except Nathalie. He pressed some kind of buttons on a picture of his wife.

He pressed the buttons and some kind of lift came from the ground and he went up. "Nooroo, dark wings rise!" said Gabrial.

He was just like the other superheroes but he was a little different. He had a dark violet costume, a silver mask covering his whole head and a long stick that could convert his butterflies into 'Akumas'.

Akumas are also some kind of butterflies but a little too dark and could convert innocent people into some kind of monsters.

Hawk Moth can convert people into villains when they are angry, sad, annoyed or disgusted at any time or day.

"Fly away my little Akuma and evilize her..". He said it in a monotonous way which felt like a command, the Akuma flew away towards Alya.

When the Akuma reached its destination, it went towards Alya's ear and was absorbed by her earring.

"Hello Alya, I am Hawkmoth... Now that people have forgotten your birthday, you can teach them a lesson, in return, you shall bring me Ladybug and Catnoir's miraculous." Said Hawk through the Akuma. "You got yourself a deal.." Some kind of blue-black liquid crawled over her body while Alya said it.

She then transformed into a villain. She tiptoed out of the classroom so that no one would notice her. But she was wrong. One of the classmates named 'Sabrina' saw her.

"Is there a fashion show going on?" Said Sabrina. "Alya, Is that you?" Said Marinette as she went a step near Alya. "Don't you dare ever think about coming near me." said Alya in panic. "You also have a special weapon called a 'birthday spoiler,' " Said Hawkmoth.

"You will be called....Birthday Spoiler." Said Hawk Moth. "That's a pretty childish name, Hawk Moth," said Alya. "No, don't listen to him" Marinette ordered her.

"Why should I stop, you're the first one who forgot my birthday, I was waiting for all of you to surprise me, alas you all forgot.." Said Birthday Spoiler as she rushed towards the exit gate of the building.

Marinette rushed to the restroom as fast as she could. "We need to transform Tikki." Said Marinette. "Ok ok, say spots on."

Tikki said in a hurry. "Tikki, Spots on." Marinette then transformed and rushed outside. Adrian too went into in locker rooms. "Plagg, Claws out!" Said Adrian.

"Wow dude, you still remember- hey! I'm not ready yet!" Cried Plagg as Adrian transformed. Both Ladybug and Catnoir met but couldn't find the Birthday Spoiler. Then, someone laughs at them in a deep voice. "Haha!! Couldn't you find me? Still tired? I guess I'm the winner here," Said Birthday Spoiler. "Never! You will never win!" Said Catnoir. Ladybug smiled at Catnoir and started to swing her yoyo.

"Ready?" Asked Ladybug. "I'm just doing this for the first time, but I'm ready!" Catnoir replied. "So you think you could win, huh? Let's see about that, haha!" Laughed Birthday Spoiler (Alya). "You people had forgotten that today was a special day! I was so excited that I would get many gifts and more things! But now everyone hates me!" Cried Birthday Spoiler.

"That's not true!" Said Ladybug. "No one hates you Alya, they just forgot your birthday, I guess?" Said Cat Noir. "Let's go back Alya!" Said Cat Noir.

"Never!" Said Alya as she swung her weapon and was about to hit Cat Noir but suddenly, she got a call from Hawkmoth. "I told you to get their miraculous! Not to chit-chat with them!" Said Hawkmoth and disconnected the call.

"Whatever! I just want to get revenge" Said Birthday Spoiler as she went to other homes and saw a boy who was celebrating his birthday with all of his friends.

"I wish my birthday was the same!" Cried Birthday Spoiler and destroyed the radio, everyone was in shock and were just gazing at her.

One of them shouted, "Ohh! Look! Another hero in our town!" "She's too strong!" Cried Ladybug as she searched for a new weapon in her yoyo.

"Aha! Found it!" Said Ladybug. "Lucky Charm!" Ladybug shouted and a bouquet of flowers dropped from the sky. She thought... "Well, I remember, Alya does love flowers, these are her favourite. I can distract her and get the Akuma!"

Thinking of this, Ladybug showed the flowers to Birthday Spoiler. She came near her and took the flowers and got distracted. "Finally!" Said Ladybug and took the object where the Akuma was hiding and broke it. Alya de-transformed. "Where am I? What happened?" Asked Alya in a shock.

"You don't have to worry about it," Said Cat Noir. "Exactly!" Said Ladybug and took Alya Home.

SIX
TRUTH OR DARE

"Oh hi, guys!" Said Alya. "I'm so bored!" Said Marinette and Alya agreed with her. "Wanna play truth or dare?" Asked Nino. "No way! I hate that game!!" Said Adrian. "Please!" Yelled Nino as he sat on the floor and joined his hands.

"Please?" Asked Nino again and again. Adrian was annoyed by it and had to agree with him. "Fine! But only once ok?" Said Adrian in a gentle voice.

"Yay! Your turn Alya!" Said Nino. "Hmmm... Maybe truth?" Said Alya. "Ok Your truth is have you ever got a good dream in which you are a killer?" Asked Nino. "Umm.. no? I guess.." Said Alya. "Ok! My turn! Marinette truth or dare?" Asked Adrian. "U-uhh... Maybe uhh..truth?" Marinette struggled.

"Um.. ok your truth is... have you ever hurt someone by mistake?" Asked Adrian. "Uhh.." Said Marinette as she nodded her head. "Ohh! So that's a yes" Said Adrian in shock. He thought of something else. "Nino truth or dare?" Asked Marinette. "Hmmm..dare!" Said Nino". Marinette had an evil smile on her face.

"Umm..did I do something wrong?" Asked Nino. "Exactly! Now I have a perfect dare for ya" Said Marinette with an evil smile. "Umm..this is gonna be bad" Whispered Alya in Nino's ears. "I dare you to go outside and dance like a swan". "What a kind dare.." Alya spoke out sarcastically. "Ugh! Fine!!" Said Nino as he went outside and climbed the fountain seat and started dancing like a swan. Everyone started looking and laughed. He was all red with embarrassment that he went inside and shouted at Marinette. But she didn't care, she was still giggling. "Stop laughing!" Said Nino.

"Oh hi, guys!" A girl named Alex came up to her and asked if she could play with them too. "Oh of course Alex!" Said Marinette.

"Thanks, Mari!" Alex replied. "Ok, truth or dare Alex?" Asked Nino. "Umm.. dare!" Said Alex. "Your dare is to take out your shoe and aim it on your locker," Said Nino.

"That's easy!" Said Alex as she took out her shoe and aimed it to her locker. Bang! There was a lot of noise but no one cared.

"Done!" Said Alex and gave Marinette a hive-five. Tring! "Welp! There goes the bell!" Said Alya. "Yeah what class do you have now?" asked Alya. "I have Math," Said Nino. "I have French," Said Alex. "Marinette and I have the same class". Said Adrian. "What is it?" asked Alex. "It's English". Said Marinette.

"Ok! Bye guys! We can continue later, bye!" Said Alya. "Ok," Said Marinette, and they went to their classes.

SEVEN

SCHOOL

Yawns "Good morning Tikki!" Said Marinette as she got up from her bed and came down. She rubbed her eyes and stretched. She looked at the calendar and gasped. "Oh no!" Marinette shouted and she started to collect her school books and took out her clothes.

"What's wrong Marinette?" Tikki asked and tried to calm Marinette down. "I had a test today! I forgot to study!" Said Marinette and packed her bag then rushed outside.

"What will you do now?" Tikki asked in a hurry. She followed Marinette and they went straight to school. "Your late Marinette!" Said the security guard. "Ooh! I'm sorry!" Marinette struggled and rushed to class. She sat on her seat which was with Alya.

"Where's Ms.Bustier?" Asked Marinette as she plucked out some branches from her head. "What's with all the sticks in your head?" Asked Alya. "Don't ask," Said Marinette.

"She's coming!" Nino said in a panic. "Did anyone study!?" Asked Alex. The whole class nodded as a 'NO'. "Good Morning class!" Said Ms.Bustier. "D-do we have a test today Ms.Bustier?" Asked Alex.

"Hmmm...no, you will have your test next Tuesday!" Said Ms.Bustier. The whole class sighed in relief. "Yes!! We are spared be god! Thank you, Jesus Christ." Said Nino and started dancing on the table. "Nino!" shouted Ms.Bustier. "Stop it!".

"Yes, ma'am," Said Nino and sat down with his hat hiding his eyes.

After a while of 'studying', the bell rang. "There goes the bell!" said Ms.Bustier and everyone ran out of the class. "Looks like everyone hates school huh?" Said Ms.Bustier whipping her sweat from her forehead. "That was tiring." Thought Ms.Bustier and stepped outside and suddenly, she heard whispering from the principal's office. Ms.Bustier peeked through the window and saw the principal talking with someone about her. Ms.Bustier bursted into tears and went crying into the restroom. And there comes Hawkmoth!

"Ahhh.. I can finally give someone the power to defeat Ladybug and Cat Noir!" Said hawkmoth and made a butterfly sit on his silver hands and covered them.

The butterfly transformed into the akuma and fluttered away from Hawkmoths' hands. "Fly away my little akuma and evilize her!" Said Hawkmoth and the akuma went flying in the air and finally reached its destination. Woosh! Ms.Bustier's beautiful blue eyes soon transformed into the weird purple butterfly.

"Hello Ms.Bustier, I am Hawkmoth," said that butterfly man again. "You now have the power to turn people into ice!" After saying that, Ms.Bustier was covered with purple liquid and transformed into an ice queen.

"You are now the Ice Queen" Said Hawkmoth, again.. "I want you to bring Ladybug and Cat Noir's miraculous" exclaimed Hawkmoth and the Ice Queen rushed around, turning people into ice. Marinette was just relaxing at home and watching the news with Tikki. Suddenly, she saw the news about the Ice Queen.

"We have to transform Tikki!" Marinette exclaimed and transformed into Ladybug and jumped out of her window. As she was jumping from one building to another, she stood up on the Museum's roof and tried to contact Cat Noir.

As with Adrian, he was just lying on his bedroom sofa and Plagg was eating his favourite food, Camembread. Outside, he saw Ladybug on the Museum's roof and thought to ask her about why she transformed. "Plagg claws out!" Adrian exclaimed and transformed into Cat Noir, but when he was transforming, he heard whispering of Plagg. Cat Noir jumped out of the window and walked up to Ladybug and Ladybug eventually saw him and ran up to him and said, "Chat! I had been contacting you for hours!"

"Sorry m'lady, I was umm.. I was-" "You were?" said Ladybug with a weird grin on her face. "I was umm.. I was dancing!" Said Cat Noir. "Dancing in Adrian's house?" Said Ladybug and continued, "I saw you in Adrian's house.. What were you doing there?" Still a grin on Ladybug's face and there comes the Ice Queen.

She laughs and was about to say something but Cat Noir stickers his leg in and breaks up the point. "Eww.. do you even brush your teeth? Your mouth smells disgusting! Even my kwami doesn't smell that much!" Cat Noir laughs and walks up to Ice Queen

"You know Elsa, you can just give up and give me the thing where the Akuma is hidden and everything is over" Cat Noir reaches his hand in front of Ice Queen.

"First of all, I'm not Elsa, I'm the Ice Queen! Second, I will give you a-" and there goes Cat Noir again, "You will give me a what?" "I will give you a-" again Cat Noir stickers his leg in,

"You will give me a treat!?" Said Cat Noir and does 'the' little puppy eyes.

"Let me say something!" yelles Ice Queen and from there, even Hawkmoth is disturbed by everything and slams his forehead. "Ice Queen! What are you doing!? I told you to get their miraculous not to have a conversation with them!" Exclaimed and the Ice Queen continued, "I will give you a kick!" Ice Queen pushes her leg behind and Cat Noir freaks out and says, "I didn't see that coming, and by the way, please don't throw me in the water!" And Ice queen kicks her leg and well there goes Cat Noir flying in the sky and says in the air, "You will pay for it Elsa!" and goes flying into the water.

"I told you- not to throw me- in the water-!" Cat Noir couldn't even say things properly as he was in the water floating and going down again and again and comes out of the water.

While with Ladybug, she started to fight with Ice Queen. She suddenly stopped, and was mumbling something. Ladybug thought that it might be Hawkmoth again. And wrapped her with her yoyo. The Ice Queen urged and moved a lot.

"Now where's the Akuma hidden?" Asked Ladybug in a crumbled tone. "Why should I tell you, huh?" Ice Queen answered. Ladybug then pulled her yoyo and made it even more tight and difficult to move. "I'm asking you the last time, "Where is the Akuma hidden?" Ladybug asked in anger.

"I still ain't tellin' ya", answered Ice Queen and froze her yoyo and finally came out. "My yoyo!" Cried Ladybug and tried one of her powers. "Lucky charm!" And what came falling down? A fork. "A fork? What am I supposed to do with this!?" Said Ladybug.

"What are you going to do with a fork? Eat noodles?" Said Ice Queen and started laughing. Ladybug thought about how to use the fork and saw that one of her bracelets were frozen and was using it in the fight. "Oh.. I don't know what to do.." Ladybug acted as if she didn't know anything and started running towards her bracelet, and SMASH!

Her bracelet broke into pieces and there runs the Akuma. "No evil doing for you little Akuma." Said Ladybug and dropped her yoyo at the end of it and started spinning it.

"Time to de-evilize" She said it again and in seconds, she caught the Akuma and let it free into the form of a normal white-glowing butterfly. As then she shouted her special ability to fix everything to normal, "Miraculous Ladybug!" Suddenly, she heard footsteps which were coming towards her. It was just Cat Noir. "Chat! You're late again!" Said Ladybug in an injured tone.

"Oh! I'm sorry m'lady!" Answered Cat Noir, "I was soaking wet and thought to stay in the sun", "Whatever" Answered Ladybug. After the argument, Ladybug and CatNoir saw that there was still a lot of ice left that the Ice Queen left behind.

"Lucky Charm!" Said Ladybug and threw her yoyo into the air and a bag of salt dropped from the air out of nowhere. "A bag of salt?" "What am I supposed to do with this?" Ladybug said as she looked beneath her and saw that the salt was coming out of the bag and was making the ice melt. "Alright kitty, I have a job for you".

"What is it, M'lady?" Cat Noir and Ladybug gave her the bag of salt to him and told him to follow her. Cat Noir followed Ladybug and the salt out of the bag was making all the ice melt.

"Alright I think we are done". Said Ladybug and took the empty bag which was full of salt and said.. "Miraculous Ladybug" As Ladybug said, she threw the empty bag and the same bag fluttered into Red linings all over Paris. "Kitty, now Cataclysm Ice Queen's Akuma's hiding place" "But M'lady we still don't know where the Akuma is hidden". Said Cat Noir and Ladybug dragged him close to Ice queen and said "Ice Queen was firing us from this stick"

"I want you to cataclysm it" Said Ladybug and Cat Noir said.."Cataclysm!" After Cat Noir said that, he touched this hand on the stick and it shattered into ashes. And there goes the Akuma! "No evil doing for you little Akuma.. Time to de-evilize!" As Ladybug said, she spinned her yoyo and caught the Akuma. "Gotcha!" Ladybug said and let the Akuma that turned into a normal butterfly, fly away.

As she let the butterfly go, the Ice Queen turned into Ms.Bustier. "Pound it!" Said Ladybug and Cat Noir and punched each other's fists and both if their Miraculouses started blinking and making certain sounds. "Oh looks like we're gonna transform back" "So what?" Said Cat noir "Oh Buggout!" Said Ladybug and left running towards a wall. "But you didn't even answer my question!" Said Cat Noir and left as well.

EIGHT
SAPOTIS

"Y-yes Ms.Siser! The girls are ready for bed! Uhh- technically speaking.. Umm yeah, they're good, enjoy the movie!" Said Marinette talking on her phone, looking at Alya and her little sisters- Ella and Etta.

"C'mon bed time you little monsters!" Said Alya while showing a dinosaur posture to her sisters, laughed and carried them both in between her arms and took them to their room to make them sleep.

"It's not us, it's the sapoties!" said those little two girls. "Well now it's bed time you little sapoties!" "You don't wanna be late for tomorrow's amusement park day!" Alya tucked them both in their blankets and touched the tip of Etta's nose, sitting on her bed.

"We don't wanna go to bed!" "Yea, we wanna stay up like you!" Said those two girls. "Well what kind of zombies will you be at the amusement park tomorrow if you go to bed late?" Said Alya and looked at Marinette who was just a few feet away, at the doorstep wearing her pyjamas.

"Show them Marinette" Said Alya and Marinette didn't hesitate to act and showed Ella and Etta how their gonna be if they do not go to bed. Marinette yawned, stretched, rubbed her eyes and laid at the side of the door. "So what's it gonna be, boring pyjama party with the big kids or the super cool fun amusement park tomorrow?" Said Alya raising her arm in the air.

"Yes, the amusement park!" Said those little girls, falling on the pillows and closing their eyes in excitement. "That's what I thought, so good night sapoties." Said Alya while taking their sister's caps. "No, can we keep them on, please?" "Alright Sapoties, then you better go to sleep" Said Alya, leaving the room, with Marinette waiting for her in the kitchen.

Alya came into the kitchen and took out a tray of orange juice, with two glasses. "So what were those sa-sopa-?" Marinette stuttered in confusion. "You mean the sapoties?" "Ya! The sapoties! Ummm- what are sapoties exactly?" Said Marinette.

"Ohh! Those little creatures! Sapoties are mischievous little monsters always looking for something to pull pranks on". As Alya said that, Marinette opened the freezer and took out a musk-mellon. "Now that we're alone, I can finally tell you, apparently Ladybug has been around at least in the pharos, no way we know that Ladybug can be five thousands years old, so.. I found this downloaded a great app that analyzes some recordings I have for talking. Based on the frequencies of her voice, it turns out that Ladybug is a girl of our age!" Marinette twitched her eyelids and pretended that she didn't know about what Alya was talking about.

"Ummm-Alya.. The orange juice..?" Said Marinette pointing towards the jug of orange juice. As Alya turned around, she saw her little sisters in the living room and saw that her sisters drank the whole jug.

Alya walked up to them and saw them with her eyebrows up and down. Alya carried them two in between her arms and was taking them back to bed. "It's not us, it's the sapoties!" Said Ella and Etta and started laughing. Alya tucked them in bed and left the room. Marinette was just taking the musk-mellon in the living room and kept it on the table. Alya came up to her. "So what were we talking about again..?"

"Uhhh..we were about to watch a movie!" Said Marinette running towards the T.V. and accidentally showed her the picture of Ladybug. Marinette looked at it and flipped it over and showed her another. "Oh yeah, Ladybug! She is like a high school girl, so to figure out who she is we need to figure out a girl our age who's always late-" And as Alya continued, Marinette put her palm on her phone and continued.. "Isn't there a good thing that she keeps her identity a secret- uhh.." As Marinette was about to finish, Alya's little sisters came into the living room giggling.

As Alya looked behind, the musk-mellon was gone, only its outer covering was left. Alya went into their sister's room stomping and opened the door harshly.

"Okay! Get out of bed one more time and no one will be going to the amusement park tomorrow!" "It's not us, it's the sapoties!" Her sisters giggled. "This is your last warning! No jokes!" Ella nodded and closed her eyes. Alya closed the door and left, she went into the kitchen with Marinette washing the dishes.

"So what were we saying about Ladybug's identity?" Alya Asked and Marinette continued.. "Ladybug needs to protect her secret identity or her family and friends will be in danger! Hawkmoth will know who she is and can even track her!" As Alya was about to begin her conversation, she heard giggling again from the living room.

Her sisters were looking for a movie to watch at the T.V. on the kid's section. Alya came in front of the T.V. and looked at them with anger.

Her sisters giggled and said it again.. "It's not us, it's the-" "Yeah, well now it's too late!" Alya carried them in between her arms and took them back to bed.

"That's it now no one is going to the amusement park tomorrow!" Said Alya, putting them back in bed and taking their caps off.

Alya rushed towards the door and slammed it shut. Those two started bringing tears in their eyes. "I don't want another peek out of you.. Wash your hands, clean your room, kids should be doing whatever they want." Said Hawkmoth and bringed his hand and got it open.

A butterfly came to his hand and Hawkmoth covered it. Some dark particles started to appear and the butterfly turned into an Akuma. "Fly away my little akuma, and evillize them!" Said Hawkmoth and the Akuma fluttered into the air.

The two sisters were fighting in their room for the cap. The Akuma went into the cap and made it all black. The two sisters got the shape of the purple butterfly. "Sapoties, I am Hawkmoth. Your big sister is telling you what to do? Well I'll let you be as mischievous as you want.". The sisters continued.

"Do whatever we want, like to stay up all night, and go to the movies, and get lots of desserts, and drink orange juice-!"

"Y-yes yes, but calm down, from now on, no one will be able to punish you because it will always be another sapoties for you, all you have to do is to get Ladybug and Cat Noir's Miraculous, and give them to your good friend Hawkmoth, okay?" Said Hawkmoth and the purple butterfly mark disappeared and instead, the same black thing started to grow all over them.

Alya and Marinette were just watching a show and started hearing giggling from their room. "That's it I have totally had it with these kids!" Said Alya and walked up to their room.

When Alya opened the door, she saw some red coloured creatures also known as 'Sapoties'. Alya yelled and fell down as the sapoties came running towards her.

They came out of the room and started eating the food that Alya and Marinette just made. Marinette stood up on the couch shouting. Those sapoties were duplicating. One was blowing bubbles in the fish tank, some were inside the refrigerator, some were making a mess on Alya's desk.

"They multiply everytime after they eat!" Said Marinette. One of the duplicate ones, pointed towards the open window.

"Marinette, the window! Don't let them out!"Alya cautioned, Marinette yelled again and ran towards the open window but it was too late. All the sapoties managed to get out of there. The sapoties jumped through the window, held a pipe, and slid down to the town. But, there were still two of them left inside. "Marinette take care of these two!", Alya said and took the stairs and ran down.

When she opened the front door, she saw a lot of sapoties, chasing other people and making a mess all around. Some were chasing other people, some were making other cars disbalanced. Marinette on the other hand, couldn't ever catch the two that were left. She came out on the balcony, and Tikki appeared from her bag. "Time to transform, Tikki Spots on!" Said Marinette and transformed into Ladybug.

"Plagg, did you see that!?" Said Adrian, he was just watching T.V. in his room and saw the news about those sapoties. "Plagg, Claws out!" Said Adrian. "But I was just about to have fun with my camembert-" Before Plagg could finish, he just got sucked up into Adrian's ring.

Cat Noir jumped out of his room's window and saw Ladybug. "It's for villains-" "To play around with traffic lights" Said Cat Noir before Ladybug could finish. Ladybug tied up the duplicate one. It came down by hanging from the traffic light's wires.

Ladybug took off it's cap and broke the tip of it. The sapote disappeared. "How did you know that we had to destroy the monster's cap?" Asked Cat Noir. "I, uhhh tried to use my brain?" Ladybug struggles a bit. "But no Akuma has been released" Said Cat Noir, "No, 'cause that monster was a clone". Said Ladybug, "These sapoties multiply, everytime they eat".

Cat Noir then went away and saw a few sapoties riding a bicycle. Cat Noir elongated his stick on the bicycle wheel and stopped it by making them flying into the air and Ladybug then spinned her yoyo and hit the duplicate sapoties and caught their caps.

Ladybug broke them into pieces. The duplicate sapoties disappeared. The sapoties were everywhere! Ladybug and Cat Noir saw a lot of duplicate sapoties were at the ice-cream stall throwing all the ice-creams on the ground.

When Ladybug and Cat Noir came closer, the sapoties saw them and there, the same purple butterfly mark appeared on their faces.

"Seize their Miraculous!" Said Hawkmoth and the sapoties started coming closer to Ladybug and Cat Noir. "Mi-ra-cu-lous!" Said the sapoties while walking towards them like a zombie that just came out of it's grave. Ladybug and Cat Noir also started running towards them and started attacking them.

Ladybug and Cat Noir came to an end of a bridge. "We can't destroy all of their caps, there's too many of them!" Said Cat Noir in a ninja posture. "Lucky Charm!" Said Ladybug and some red glitters started to appear. A teapot came falling down from the sky. Cat Noir went to attack the sapoties while Ladybug looked around to get some ideas about how to use the teapot at fights.

"Wait! I know someone who can help! Got to go!" Said Ladybug and turned around. "Wait, right now!?" Said Cat Noir. "Cat Noir you gotta' trust me on this one!" Said Ladybug and swung her yoyo and went jumping on the top of the buildings. She then went home and saw another box of a Miraculous.

She opened it and saw an orange fox-tail looking pendant. Ladybug jumped outside and went to Alya's house. As Ladybug entered, Alya was shocked. "Oh my gosh, Ladybug! What are you doing here?"

"Alya Césaire, here is the Miraculous of the fox. It grants you the power of illusions. You must use it for the greater good. Once the job is done, you must return the miraculous to me. Can I trust you on this?" Before Ladybug could finish, Alya began.. "You can count on me Ladybug!"

Ladybug gave Alya the box and she opened it. She saw a bright light coming out of it and saw a fox-Kwami. "Hello, I am Trixx. I am your new Kwami. You just have to say, 'Trixx, let's pounce!'"

"Trixx, let's pounce!" Said Alya and began to transform. "So awesome! But why do I look like a weird animal in this".

"Come on Alya, we got some villains to fight." Both of them rushed and jumped on the buildings". Cat Noir as well, was still fighting the villains.

He jumped on a building top and saw Ladybug. "M'lady!" Said Cat Noir and rushed towards her. "Hey Chat. I bought a friend as well with me". "Woah, who's this?" Asked Cat Noir. "I'm.. I'm Rena Rouge! Yeah, I'm Rena Rouge!" Said Alya. "So I was right, there are more than two Miraculouses! Seize their Miaculouses! They are nothing against you all!" Said Hawkmoth on the other hand.

All of the sapoties across Paris started running towards Cat Noir, Ladybug and Rena Rouge. The three came down and started to spin their weapons for protection.

Ladybug spinned her yoyo, Cat Noir spinned his stick while Rena Rouge was just looking at her weapon which was a flute. She started to spin that as well. "We're surrounded by these monsters.

"We're retreating" Said Ladybug and started running towards a wall. Cat Noir pulled Rena Rouge and the three of them jumped on the top of the wall. There was no escape. The sapoties could also climb walls. "Woah, there must be thousands of them!" Said Cat Noir.

"Lucky Charm!" Ladybug recited and red sparkles appeared. A unicycle appeared from the sky and dropped in her arms. She looked around to get some clues on how to use it. She saw that a few of the duplicate sapoties were riding a rickshaw. She also saw a bin, and a truck, with a few racks in it. She looked around for more items.

She saw traffic cones, then looked around to Cat Noir's stick, and Rena Rouge's flute. And at last, she looked at the unicycle which was in her arms. After Ladybug had gotten ideas, she saw a lot of the sapoties were now climbing another building which was just beside the three.

"Whenever you're ready m'lady". Said Cat Noir and jumped off, Rena Rouge as well. Ladybug jumped down and spinned her yoyo and wrapped it around the bin that she saw earlier. She wrapped around the traffic cone, and all the things that she saw earlier. "Unicycle wheel, bin, traffic cones, are these all necessary to save Paris?" Asked Rena Rouge from another wall. She came up to Ladybug and Cat Noir as well.

"Trust me Rena Rouge". Said Ladybug. Cat Noir lowered his stick and elongated it at the end of a bridge. Ladybug and Rena Rouge took the bin which was full of Ladybug's supplies which she created by her hawk eyes and where transported through Cat Noir's stick, to the other side of the bridge.

Ladybug sat on the rickshaw and started speaking through the traffic cone. "The sapotie land has an amusement park which is about to open!" Ladybug exclaimed frankly.

All the sapoties saw her and followed. Cat Noir also saw her doing this and went bouncing towards Rena Rouge.

"Alright Rena Rouge, time to use your power". Said Cat Noir. "But I've never tried it, I hope it works". Rena Rouge credenced. "Just think of an illusion you want to create, stay focused".Cat Noir filled her with faith.

Rena Rouge nodded and began. She played her flute in a tune. "Mirage!" she exclaimed and aimed it towards an empty area. The illusion that she imagned was a big, bright amusement park; her illusion came to life. The sapoties saw the amusement park and started running towards it. "Awesome!" Said Rena Rouge. Suddenly, her necklace started to flash. The first orange light had disappeared. "My necklace is flashing, that means I'm gonna change back soon, right?" Asked Rena Rouge.

"Yeah, but don't worry, I can keep a secret". Rena Rouge tucked her flute at the back, "You know our identities must remain a secret".

"Good job, you're a fast learner".Cat Noir was proud. "If you need any superhero tips, you know where it comes from". Said Rena Rouge.

Ladybug was still speaking about the amusement park to make all the sapoties follow her towards the illusion.

"No! Don't go there! Ladybug has found a way to trap you!" Hawkmoth warned the Sapoties. Ladybug came into a narrow path and stopped.

"It's upto Cat Noir, now!" Ladybug yelled and jumped up. The wheel was now a hat picker. The racks which were one of Ladybug's ideas, it's sticks were removed and only the spiky area was left.

The spiky area was then attached to the wheel and was taped at the edge of the wheel. The wheel was lowered down and Cat Noir stuck his stick in the middle to make it spin. Cat Noir's stick made the wheel get stuck in between the walls of the narrow way.

Cat Noir spinned the wheel and the caps of the sapoties were being collected. They were stocked in the same bin. After they got all the caps, Cat Noir got his Cataclysm and cataclysme the bin. All the duplicate sapoties disappeared. The two, 'Ella and Etta' were also back to normal. Ladybug saw the Akuma flying away. "No evil doing for you little Akuma". "Time to de-evilize!" Ladybug recited and spinned her yoyo and caught the Akuma. "Gotcha!"

Ladybug tapped on her yoyo's surface and a white butterfly flew away. "Bye bye little butterfly". Ladybug lifted the wheel and threw it in the air. "Miraculous Ladybug!" Said Ladybug and red sparkles started to appear. Everything was back to normal.

Rena Rouge removed the illusion of the amusement park. Rena Rouge was about to jump just when she looked behind, Ladybug and Cat Noir were waiting for her to do the ending with the 'pound it'.

Rena Rouge came up to them. "Pound it!" the three exclaimed in excitement. Rena Rouge's miraculous was almost out of energy. It's last bit was flashing.

Ladybug took Rena Rouge to an area where no one could see. Rena Rouge de-transformed into Alya again. Ladybug bringed out her hand and wanted the fox miraculous back. But Alya didn't want to.

"Alya, we made a promise". Said Ladybug and her earrings were flashing as well. She ran towards a door and closed it. She de-transformed into her real form again too. Alya thought about it and opened the door slightly. Marinette was now a bit far away from the door's openings.

Alya kept the miraculous box on the ground and ran away. Marinette looked at the miraculous and smiled.

While with Cat Noir...

He had to deal with the little girls, Ella and Etta. Cat Noir had to carry them in his arms and bring them back home. He left the girls in their room and left.

NINE

JAGGED STONE

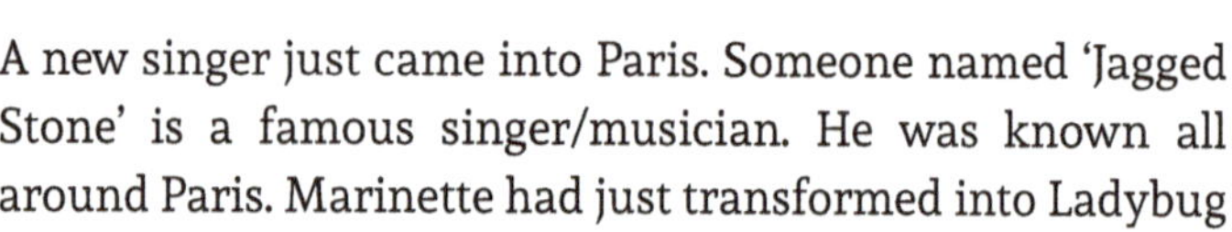

A new singer just came into Paris. Someone named 'Jagged Stone' is a famous singer/musician. He was known all around Paris. Marinette had just transformed into Ladybug and was having an ordinary afternoon with nothing to do.

She hopped about, jumped and swung over buildings. She came home and de-transformed.

"I'm so tired Tikki". Said Marinette, slammed her head with her pillow. "Well you shouldn't have just wasted your energy in just jumping around like that". Tikki replied.

"I know Tikki, but the safety of Paris is more important". Said Marinette and fell on her bed and was about to have some rest until her father called her from downstairs. "Marinette! Could you help us in the bakery?".

"Ugh.. I just wanted to have some rest.." Marinette spoke up to herself with a big frown on her face.

She went downstairs and helped her parents bake some cookies. A man with purple and faded with black coloured hair entered.

"Jagged Stone?" Tom asked as if he just realized something.

"Well rock-and-roll people!" Said that purple headed man. "Mom, you know him, and how does dad know him?" Marinette asked in hesitation.

"Marinette, this is Jagged Stone! He is a well known singer here in Paris!" Sabine replied. "Umm.." Marinette stood there, staring at him. "So, he's a singer?" She continued asking questions.

Her father was talking with Jagged Stone while Marinette got bored. "I wanna get out of here Tikki!" Marinette whispered to Tikki, making sure that no one was listening.

"What was that, Marinette?" Sabine asked. Marinette had her intentions wrong. She looked around, panicking. "On, nothing... I was just saying that we should open up the windowsso that the fumes of the cookies can escape" Marinette stuttered. "Oh that's no worries Marinette". Said Sabine. "Ahh! Is this your daughter, Tom?" Asked Jagged Stone.

"Why yes, this is Marinette!" Said Tom and pushed Marinette in front of Jagged Stone.

"Well rock-and-roll Marinette! I am Jagged Stone and I am gonna be your new favourite singer!" Jagged Stone said as if he was really 'over-confident'. Marinette smiled in hesitation. Marinette stood there, not uttering a single word. Her parents then pushed her aside to talk to Jagged Stone. She had no other task to do so she just went upstairs, back to her room. She sat on her chair and Tikki came out of her pocket. "Marinette, you need to gain confidence" Tikki advised. "I can't Tikki, I don't know why I just mix up my words a lot, so this time, I just stayed quiet." Said Marinette. She then got up in a hurry.

"Tikki spots on!" Marinette recited. She jumped out of the window and swung her yoyo and wrapped it around a building's pole and glided towards it. She looked through the building's windows and jumped on and across many more buildings.

She came home in the evening, de-transformed and went downstairs. "Marinette! Where were you?" Said Sabine who was in a bad mood. "Uh mom, I just fell asleep in the bathroom!" Marinette stuttered and finally got an excuse.

"Well you should have woken up". Said Sabine. Marinette apologized and went back upstairs and fell on her bed.

"Marinette, why have you been out for so long?"Tikki was quite concerned.

"I was just bored, okay?" Marinette raged a bit. "Marinette, dinner's ready!" Said Sabine from downstairs. "Coming mom!" Marinette replied.

"Well you better not keep them waiting or you might again look for an excuse". Said Tikki. "Yeah, yeah, Tikki". Said Marinette and gave Tikki a macaron.

She went downstairs to have dinner while Tikki had finished the macaron and fell asleep.

TEN

NADIA CHAMAK

"Yeah, I guess you should first just take a try out". Said one of the news reporters at the T.V. station. "Hi, I'm Nadia Chamak and I'm here to get this job as a news reporter". Said Nadia Chamak who wanted to become a news reporter for years.

The T.V. station workers were first gonna take a try out then filming. "Alright, three, two, one start!" Said one of the station workers. "Don't be amused, it's just the news! Today we're gonna have a face-to-face live stream with Ladybug and Cat Noir! Tonight!" Said Nadia.

"Alright Nadia, that was fine. Now let's film it". Said one of the workers. "Don't be amused, it's just the news! Today we're gonna have a face-to-face live stream with Ladybug and Cat Noir, tonight!" Nadia said it again.

The news reporter uploaded it on the news and everyone in Paris had heard it. And there lies Marinette, sewing her purse which had a hole at the bottom. Tikki saw the news and was in shock. "Marinette, you need to hear this".

"Isn't it great, Tikki? Cat Noir and I can help another news reporter who wants to become one, Marinette replied. "But Marinette! It's tonight!" "Wait, tonight?" Marinette stuttered.

"Yes tonight!" "I can't, Tikki! I have babysitting!" Said Marinette and picked up her phone and called Alya to come over.

When she came over, Marinette explained that she had to babysit and needed some help.

"Oh! I can help you with that! I'm always free for my best friend!" Said Alya and sat down.

Marinette put a mattress on the floor and put her computer down. She suddenly heard the doorbell ring. Marinette ran down stairs and opened the front door.

"Oh, Nadia Chamak! I saw your ad on the live stream with Ladybug and Cat Noir!" Said Marinette.

"Why thank you for seeing my ad, and this is my daughter, Manon. You are going to babysit her" Said Nadia Chamak.

"Okay, I'll do that". Marinette replied.

"Alright Marinette, Manon has already had dinner". "No problem, Nadia. You go and take care of the show, good luck with that!" Marinette cheered her up.

"Thank you Marinette". Said Nadia Chamak and left". Marinette brought Manon upstairs. "Marinette, are you babysitting Manon?" Asked Alya.

"Yeah, you know her?" Asked Marinette as well. "Of course we know each other". "Alya!" Said Manon and ran towards her. Alya switched on the computer and watched the news of Ladybug and Cat Noir.

"Umm.. Alya, I have to tell my bakery something, their in the parents" Marinette jumblemed her words. "You mean tell your parents something in the bakery?" Alya fixed up for her.

At the T.V. station, Nadia was sitting on the couch in front of the camera, and Cat Noir hopped in and sat on the couch in front of her. "W-woah!" Nadia almost dropped her i-pad while stuttering.

"From which way did you come in?" Asked Nadia. "Super Celebrities's ways". Cat Noir replied. "Ladybug is coming late I guess". Said Cat Noir.

While Marinette finally got an excuse to become Ladybug and go for her interview. "Tikki spots on!" Said Marinette and transformed into Ladybug.

She rushed outside and swung her yoyo, wrapped it around one of the building's top and swung across the roads, houses and jumped on the top of the T.V. station.

Ladybug slammed the door open and swung her yoyo and wrapped it around the pole on the roof. She jumped and landed in front of Nadia Chamak.

The T.V. station workers started the camera and Nadia continued. "Don't be amused, it's just the news! Today we are going to have a face-to-face conversation with our best superheroes, Ladybug and Cat Noir!"

"That's very nice of you Nadia to have us here!" Said Cat Noir showing a weird smile. "Uhh... yeah, it's a pleasure to have you both too". Said Nadia.

"So, Ladybug and Cat Noir, have you ever revealed your identity to anyone yet?" Asked Nadia.

"Well, no one knows it because our identities must remain a secret!" Ladybug replied.

"Then why don't you show it to us! We can keep it a secret". Said Nadia.

"No Nadia, we can't! Who knows about who the super villain can be! No one knows who he is, where he is, and why he is doing this!" Ladybug replied with a frown on her face.

"So do you both know each other's identities then?" Nadia asked again.

"No, we don't. We aren't supposed to know each other's identities. No one can." Ladybug spoke up calmly.

"Then tell us more about you!" Exclaimed Nadia.

"Nadia, we're superheroes, not stars! We should be doing our job, not looking like fools on T.V." Said Ladybug and left the studio.

Cat Noir apologised to Nadia about everything and rushed outside too.

Nadia sighed and left the studio.

On the other hand...

Gabriel Agreste was watching the news as well. He said to himself.. "Such pure pain, a perfect victim for my plan..".

www.ingramcontent.com/pod-product-compliance
Lightning Source LLC
Chambersburg PA
CBHW040111150726
48005CB00013B/1654